D0810238

Created by Jim Jinkins

Doug's™
Journal

Adapted by Sue Kassirer

Illustrated by
Pete List
Cheng-li Chan
Tony Curanaj
Chris Dechert
Brian Donnelly
Ray Favata
Chris Palesty
Matthew C. Peters
Doris Santos
Michael Zodorozny
Jeff Nodelman

JUMBO®
PICTURES
INC.

GRADE A QUALITY

DISNEP
PRESS

New York

Copyright © 1997 by Disney Enterprises, Inc.

Original Characters for " The Funnies" Developed
by Jim Jinkins and Joe Aaron.

All rights reserved. No part of this book may be reproduced or transmitted in
any form or by any means, electronic or mechanical, including photocopying,
recording, or by any information storage and retrieval system, without written
permission from the publisher. For information address Disney Press,
114 Fifth Avenue, New York, New York 10011-5690.
Printed in the United States of America.

FIRST EDITION

10 9 8 7 6 5 4 3

The artwork for this book is prepared using watercolors and pen.

The text for this book is set in 14-point August.

Library of Congress Catalog Card Number: 97-67190

ISBN 0-7868-4154-0

Hey guys!

Hey, it's me, Doug. I guess most of you know that I keep a journal. I mean, every kid should have a journal. I have my regular human friends, Patti and Skeeter, and even my parents to talk to, but sometimes I just want to talk in a place where I can say anything I want.

I thought it might help get you started with your own journal if I showed you some of the stuff I've written in *my* journal. When I want to doodle Quailman zapping Klotzilla with his powerful Quaileye, or I want to write a new song for my top secret garage band, this is the place I like to do it, because there are no rules here, no grades. . . . This isn't homework, it's fun!

Your friend,

DOUG

All About Me

Dear Journal,

   My name is Doug Funnie. I'm twelve years old, and I live with my mom and dad and sisters, Judy and Cleopatra Dirtbike, in this town called Bluffington. My birthday is August 22. My best nonhuman friend is my dog, Porkchop. Oh, I have a best human friend, too: Skeeter. And then there is Patti Mayonnaise—I've got a secret crush on her. . . . At least I hope it's a secret.

"How did I get into this mess?"
—Doug Funnie

*What about you? Jot down some facts
about yourself here.*

Did you know?

Porkchop is exactly the same height as the famous Frenchman, Napoleon Bonaparte, but unlike Napoleon, Porkchop is more interested in Peanutty Buddies than world conquest.

Did you know?
Doug is the cartoonist on the school newspaper, *The Weekly Beebe.*

Did you know?
Doug created a dance called the Slug Hop when Roger, dressed like a hammer, accidentally banged Doug's foot at the school dance.

9

My Family

Dear Journal,

Sometimes having a baby sister isn't easy. I mean, none of us gets any sleep anymore. She throws her toys on the ground all the time, but when she boogies down, it makes it all worthwhile.

Do you have any brothers or sisters?
Get your feelings about them off your chest!

Did you know?

Doug's baby sister is named Cleopatra Dirtbike Funnie. Doug gave her her middle name. He thought he was making a list of Christmas presents he wanted. She was born on Christmas Day!

Did you know?

Skeeter Valentine has a little brother named Dale. Dale's favorite activities are playing with his food and sandbox reconnaissance. Unfortunately he thinks Doug's name is "Big Nose."

Dear Journal,

Judy is *not* a normal sister. Why can't she just be regular? I always feel like she's going to embarrass me in front of the whole world. She's gotten me to be in another one of her weird plays. Okay, fine, maybe not the end of the world, but then I find out I have to wear funny pants!

"Surely you jest, Dougie!" –Judy Funnie

"Stay out of my room! Don't touch my stuff!" —Judy Funnie

"Gather ye rosebuds! The sands of time are running apace!"—Judy Funnie

"Dougie, you are such a yokel."—Judy Funnie

Dear Journal,

Judy said, "You need to center, collect, look within!" What was I supposed to do? I could barely move my neck in that getup. I mean, how do **you** look within a cheese sandwich?

Write about your most embarrassing moments. It's good therapy.

_____

_____

_____

_____

_____

_____

_____

_____

_____

_____

_____

"Come on, Funnies!" —Phil Funnie

Did you know?

Doug's mom, Theda, has been known to work under the car—on a dolly! She works part-time at Dejavu, the local co-op recycling center. They recycle just about anything, including that thing that passes for hair on Mayor White's head. She likes to eat peanut butter turkey-toes.

"Douglas, you're not my little baby anymore.
You're a . . . young man, boo-hoo."—Theda Funnie

Dear Journal,

I guess maybe I'm sorta lucky; my dad's a great guy. He always does fun stuff with me. Like sometimes he lets me come to work with him at the Busy Beaver Department Store photo department—that's his job. I get to jiggle the Busy Beaver to make the babies smile, that kinda thing. . . .

What are your parents like?

_____

_____

_____

_____

_____

_____

_____

"I'm proud of you, mister!" —Phil Funnie

Did you know?

Doug's dad, Phil, likes to go fly-fishing. He wore bell-bottoms and danced to disco music when he was a teenager. He considered himself very groovy . . . whatever that means.

25

My Friends

Dear Journal,

Sometimes my friends make me feel so happy. . . .

Remember the happy times with your friends?

Did you know?
Beebe Bluff has a TV that fills one whole wall of her bedroom! A bazillion channels!

Did you know?
Chalky Studebaker is the top athlete
and top student in his class.

Dear Journal,

Sometimes my friends make me feel so crazy. . . .

How about the times your friends make you crazy?

_____

_____

_____

_____

_____

_____

_____

_____

_____

_____

_____

_____

"I hate shallow, snooty people; they're so shallow and snooty."–Doug Funnie

Did you know?

Al and Moo Sleech are dedicated to a search for extraterrestrial life and getting girls.

Dear Journal,

Hey, Doug again. My best friends, a great movie (*Roller Coaster Insanity*), two tubs of popcorn, soda–what more could a guy want? Ugh . . . maybe some Pepto.

Do you have a best human friend?

_____

_____

_____

_____

_____

_____

_____

_____

Did you know?
Skeeter's father is a retired tugboat captain.

Did you know?

Patti Mayonnaise loves dirt biking.

Dear Journal,

Sometimes I wish that Roger and his gang would just lay off for once—or move to another planet!

Have you ever had trouble with a bully?
How did you solve the problem?

Dear Journal,

Roger Klotz has the longest limo of any kid in town. Well, okay, he's the only kid with a limo, but still it's pretty lame. It doesn't even have one of those full-size retractable arcade video games inside. All cool limos have those; at least, mine would. Roger is just so uncool. . . . I'm not jealous . . . honest.

My Nonhuman Friends

Dear Journal,

It's good to have a nonhuman friend, especially one like Porkchop that knows how to cha-cha.

Sometimes, nonhuman friends are the best.

_____

_____

_____

_____

_____

_____

_____

_____

_____

_____

_____

_____

_____

_____

_____

_____

_____

_____

_____

_____

_____

_____

Did you know?

Porkchop lives at 21-A Jumbo Street, a tepee in the Funnies' backyard. He gets more mail than the Funnies do!

Did you ever have a pet dog who was jealous?

Did you know?
Porkchop likes to read *Dog's Life* magazine and *Bone of Fortune*.

_____

_____

_____

_____

_____

_____

_____

_____

_____

_____

_____

_____

_____

_____

_____

"Pets aren't toys; pets are people. Not people people, just nonhuman people."
—Doug Funnie

Did you know?

Mr. Dink has a remote-control dog that he just upgraded with new software—very expensive and fully operational in the rain.

Did you know?

Roger thought his cat, Stinky, was a boy until "he" had a litter of kittens.

My Hobbies

Dear Journal,

   Playing the banjo is good for taking your mind off your troubles, entertaining friends, and adding a strange, twisted element to the school marching band that always leaves the opposing team baffled and stupefied.

List of things I like to do:

Playing banjo and air guitar to The Beets

Talking to Patti Mayonnaise

Having fun with Porkchop

Playing barnyard chess

Listening to Patti Mayonnaise

Drawing cartoons

Going to the movies

Thinking about Patti Mayonnaise

Writing in my journal

Making lists in my journal

Oh yeah, did I mention Patti Mayonnaise?

Things **you** like to do:

_____

_____

_____

_____

_____

_____

_____

_____

_____

_____

_____

_____

_____

Did you know?

Patti loves to exercise. Beebe's still trying to figure out how to pay someone to do it for her.

_____

_____

_____

_____

_____

_____

_____

_____

_____

_____

_____

_____

Did you know?

Skeeter likes to invent things, but the crucial "usefulness factor" has eluded him.

Did you know?

Beebe Bluff's hobby is shopping, shopping, and shopping!

Did you know?

Now that Roger's rich he's developed some classy ideas. Now he only hangs out with sophisticated losers.

My School

Dear Journal,

Ms. Kristal sure pours on the homework. Sometimes I think I'll never get through it, and I wish she would just give us a break. But once I'm done, it's worth it. I mean, after I get through a tough assignment I can almost feel my brain expanding—it's so cool!

What are your favorite subjects and who are your favorite teachers in school?

47

"It takes a lot of practice to be
good at something, and twice as much
if you're not."—Doug Funnie

"I hear middle school is so hard that
when they give you a test, they don't even
give you the questions!" —Skeeter Valentine

Dear Journal,

Going to a school that's shaped like Beebe Bluff's head isn't so bad, but sometimes in science class I think, Ugh, I'm in Beebe's nose.

What is your school like?
Do you have science class in a nose?

_____

_____

_____

_____

_____

_____

_____

_____

_____

Did you know?
Doug's old school collapsed from termites!

Did you know?
Doug's school is called Beebe Bluff Middle School because Beebe's father paid to build it.

Did you know?

Bob White, the principal of Beebe Bluff Middle School, never gets Doug's name right. He usually calls him "Dan" or "Young person."

Having Fun

Dear Journal,

You never know what's going to be the most fun until it happens. Like the other night Skeeter and I went outside, and there were all these fire-flies. So we caught a few in a jar. It was cool watching them bounce around, blinking on and off like little flashlights. Of course Skeeter knew the Latin name for them. The guy's a genius! Really! Anyway, we let them go. I don't know what it was, but I think I'll always remember that night.

Want to remember something forever?
Write it down.

Vacations and Camp

Dear Journal,

It seems like everyone's going to camp—except me! Today Patti told me she's going to Sports Camp. Now I really want to go there, too, 'cause she's gonna be there. But the truth is, I'm terrible at sports. I don't know what to do. If I don't go, I don't get to see Patti all summer. But if I go, I risk making a fool of myself on the basketball court. . . .

Summer camp can be cool.
Write about yours!

Dear Journal,

They said it couldn't be done, but today Skeeter and I scaled the Cliffs of Insanity!

Have you ever accomplished something you thought was impossible?

_____

_____

_____

_____

_____

_____

_____

_____

_____

_____

_____

"With practice and teamwork, you can do anything!"–Doug Funnie

Dear Journal,

Tomorrow is the annual Bluffscouts
Shindigarama. Hecka-pecka-washarag.
Skin-a-dally-do! Sauerbraten,
liverwurst, sweet
patootie stew!
Bluffscouts!
Bluffscouts!
Shin-diga-diga-rama!

Did you know?

Some of the best lakes in the Bluffington area are Chowderhead Lake, Lucky Duck Lake, Rabbit's Foot Lake, and Lake Ocabago. They're great for vacations, goofing around with your friends, and hiding out—if you're a lake monster. GLORB.

Dear Journal,

I just found out today that Al and Moo Sleech are going to Virtual Camp this summer. I don't know what that means exactly, but it sounds pretty . . . virtual. They say that they get to win every event and short-sheet beds from the comfort of their own living room—no pesky reality to get in the way.

Don't you wish vacations could last forever?

Holidays

Dear Journal,

   What's wrong with my family? Don't they have any holiday spirit? Sure, they're all excited about the new baby coming and everything, but does that mean they have to forget Christmas entirely? They haven't even gotten a tree yet. . . .

If only every day was Christmas or Thanksgiving or any favorite holiday.

Did you know?

Al and Moo Sleech like to dress up in Christmas tree lights for the holidays. They say it's festive and can help keep you warm on those extra cold days.

Did you know?

In Yakkestonia people bob for apples, eat cotton candy, and trick-or-treat for Christmas. Halloween is when a giant bunny comes to hide eggs! And on Valentine's Day they clog dance with wooden shoes!

Did you know?

One year Porkchop gave Doug a new journal for Christmas.

"Christmas isn't just a tree and presents—it's more like a feeling. A feeling that's pretty hard to get by yourself."–Doug Funnie

Growing Up

Dear Journal,

Growing up is a pain. It's like sneakers that are stinky and ripped up but they're your favorite pair and you don't want new ones ever, but your mom makes you get new ones anyway because it's the first day of school. Perfect.

What do you think is the hardest part about growing up?

Driving a car.

"The only way not to worry if people thought I was grown-up or not, was to . . . not worry if people thought I was grown-up or not."—Doug Funnie

"Being grown-up means not trying to be what other people think you should be." —Doug Funnie

Dear Journal,

Sometimes there's all kinds of stuff to write about, and other times there just doesn't seem to be much. Like today: I first thought, Oh, I got up, ate breakfast, and went to school. How is that different from yesterday? Or the day before that? But then I realized that every day there's different stuff. Like today Roger said he had a hair growing on his chin. You could kind of see it, if you squinted really hard. You know, when you look extra hard there's always something cool to see, like . . . what's that? . . . Oh no! A zit! I got a zit on my nose!

You can write about anything here!

79

Love and Stuff

Dear Journal,

   Even Roger Klotz thinks I have a crush on
Patti. I don't understand why people say that.
I mean, I think about her all the time, I want to
be with her just about every second, but I don't
have a crush on her or anything like that. I mean,
she's Patti, the person I think about night and
day—it's not anything serious. A crush is like
a disease or something. I don't have that.

Is there someone you secretly like?
Keep it secret here.

_____

_____

_____

_____

_____

_____

"Love makes it hard to think." –Doug Funnie

Dear Journal,

Okay, okay, okay . . . fine. Maybe Patti likes Guy Graham. He's good-looking, he's an upperclassman, he's popular, smooth, funny. But I don't get it; what could she possibly see in him?

Did you know?
Patti Mayonnaise doesn't know that Doug is in love with her!

S.S. PATTI

Did you know?
Moo Sleech has a crush on Judy.
So does Roger!

Daydreams and Fantasies

Dear Journal,

Sometimes when something seems a little scary, or when I just don't know what to do about something, I imagine that I'm this amazing guy from Planet Bob—Quailman! When I'm Quailman, I can do anything!

Do you ever imagine you're someone else?

Did you know?

The belt on Quailman's head might look like a regular old leather belt with a regular old buckle, but it's really the quail crown, which bestows the powers of the quail on Quailman.

If you were a superhero, what would your special powers be?

_____

_____

_____

_____

_____

_____

_____

_____

_____

_____

_____

"I may not be big, but I *am* small." –Quailman

Did you know?

On Quailman's costume, the underwear-on-the-outside thing (they're actually power briefs) is an ancient dress ritual only understood by superheroes—don't ask. The cape? Come on, what superhero could resist that cool fluttering look as they effortlessly zip through the sky?

Did you know?
Quailman's sidekick is Quaildog.

Did you know?
The powers of the quail are patience, intelligence, and speed to bob and dart away from danger. And if that fails, there's the Quaileye, which leaves victims helpless and stupefied.

Did you know?
Doug's favorite comic book hero is
Man-o'-Steel Man.

Dear Journal,

Everyone says I have an overactive imagination. But sometimes it's like Patti really *is* perfect and Roger really *is* bad. I know it's probably not true, but hey, what do I know? I'm just a kid.